Stinkbomb & Ketchup-Face

Kids love these books

'Warning: side effects include tears of laughter, crazy laughing, and aching cheeks!'
CHARLOTTE

Brave heroes, evil and wicked bad guys, and an entire army called Malcolm the Cat.

Loads of books in the series . . . and still more to come.
Yippeeeeeeee!

Grown-ups love them too!

'Clever, surprising and satisfyingly silly.'
BOOKTRUST

Really, really, reallly, really, really, really (you get the idea) really funny—really!

Other books about
Stinkbomb & Ketchup-Face:

'And I'm in them too . . .
or maybe I'm not . . . ;
or perhaps I am . . . ;

Stinkbomb
&
Ketchup-Face
and the Badness of Badgers

Stinkbomb
&
Ketchup-Face
and the Quest for the
Magic Porcupine

Stinkbomb
&
Ketchup-Face
and the Evilness of Pizza

John Dougherty

Stinkbomb & Ketchup-Face

and the Bees of Stupidity

Illustrated by
David Tazzyman
(Illustrator of
Mr Gum)

OXFORD
UNIVERSITY PRESS

OXFORD
UNIVERSITY PRESS

Great Clarendon Street, Oxford OX2 6DP
Oxford University Press is a department of the University of Oxford.
It furthers the University's objective of excellence in research, scholarship,
and education by publishing worldwide

Oxford is a registered trade mark of Oxford University Press
in the UK and in certain other countries

Database right Oxford University Press (maker)

First published 2015

British Library Cataloguing in Publication Data

Data available

ISBN: 978-0-19-274273-5

1 3 5 7 9 10 8 6 4 2

Printed and bound by CPI Group (UK) Ltd, Croydon, CR0 4YY
Paper used in the production of this book is a natural,
recyclable product made from wood grown in sustainable forests
The manufacturing process conforms to the environmental
regulations of the country of origin

It goes without saying, though not without buns,
but I'm going to say it anyway.
For Noah and Cara, with all my love.

And for Millie, Fred & Bertie,
with thanks for the loan of Ziggy & Wiggo. J.D.

For Reuben & Juliette,
the stinkiest stinkers I know x. D.T.

Ye isle of
Great Kerfuffle

N

W

E

S

Toy shop

Jail

Library

Sports shop

Loose Chippings

Stinkbomb & Ketchup-Face's house

Stupidity

Mountains
of Doom

Valley of Despair

Bus
stop

Royal Palace

About Stinkbomb & Ketchup-Face and all their friends

A is for Army. And also for Annoying.
Malcolm the Cat is the entire army of Great Kerfuffle.
Yes, I know; he's just a cat.

B is for Badgers. And for Bad Guys.
The badgers are the bad guys in these stories. There are
lots of them, and they come up with evil and wicked plans.
This is because they are evil and wicked.

C is for Can't Think of Anything in the Stories
which begins with C.

D is for Dear Me, I Can't Think of
Anything in the Stories that Begins
with D, either.

E is for Evil and Wicked.
That would be the badgers again.

F is for Felicity.
Felicity is not in this story so you don't need to know about her.

G is for Great Kerfuffle.
Stinkbomb and Ketchup-Face and all of their friends live on Great Kerfuffle. It is a very silly place.

H is for Heroes.
Stinkbomb & Ketchup-Face are the heroes of this story. They are brother and sister, and they are noble and kind and good and heroic. Sometimes they are even a little bit clever.

I is for Island.
Great Kerfuffle is an island. It has a very interesting history, which you can read about in *Stinkbomb & Ketchup-Face and the Badness of Badgers*.

J is for Jail.
The badgers spend a lot of time in jail. That's because they are the bad guys.

K is for King.
King Toothbrush Weasel is the King of all of Great Kerfuffle. He is a bit daft, to be honest.

L is for Library.
The library is the most important building in all of Great Kerfuffle. Libraries are like that.

M is for Malcolm the Cat.
Or perhaps it isn't.
Or maybe it is . . .

N is for Ninja Librarian.
Miss Butterworth is a ninja librarian.
She is wise and kind and brave and
clever and not at all like a badger.

**O is for Oh, Dear, the Badgers Have Escaped from Prison
Again and are Up to No Good.**
That happens a lot.

P is for Porcupine.
One of the books is about the famous
Magic Porcupine, who lives in the little
village of Stupidity.

Q is for Quills.
Porcupines have quills.

R is for Rong.
Rong is the wrong way to spell wrong. So that's wrong. And it
doesn't have anything to do with Stinkbomb & Ketchup-Face,
either; so that's completely wrong. Why are we even talking about it?

S is for Shopping Trolley. And Starlight.
This is the little shopping trolley, who is not a horse and who is
not called Starlight, whatever Ketchup-Face may tell you.

T is for Thwart.

Stinkbomb and Ketchup-Face are very good at thwarting the badgers' evil and wicked plans.

U is for Up to No Good.

Badgers again.

V is for Very Nearly at the End of the Alphabet Now, and Then We Can Get On with the Story.

W is for Wicked.

Yep. You guessed it. Badgers.

X is for Xylophone.

There are no xylophones in any of the Stinkbomb & Ketchup-Face stories so far. But, honestly, what else begins with X? Apart from X-Ray, and there are none of those in the stories either. And xiphisternum, but that's just getting silly.

Y is for You, and Yes.

You are reading a book about Stinkbomb & Ketchup-Face right now. Yes, you are.

Z is for Zero.

Zero is the number of books that have Stinkbomb & Ketchup-Face but no badgers. It is also the number of letters of the alphabet that are left before we have finished this bit and can get on with *Stinkbomb & Ketchup-Face and the Bees of Stupidity*.

chapter 1

In which there are eventually badgers

It was a dark and stormy night on the little island of Great Kerfuffle, except that it wasn't dark or stormy.

And it wasn't night either. But that's not the point. The point is that it was the sort of night when **evil** and **wicked** things happen.

Or, at least, it *would* have been the sort of night when **evil** and **wicked** things happen, if it had been night. But it wasn't.

Look, shall we try again?

It was a rather nice evening on the little island of Great Kerfuffle. However, even though it was not dark, or stormy, or night, the badgers were plotting.

The badgers were the most **evil** and **wicked** badgers in all of Great Kerfuffle, which wasn't hard since they were also the only badgers in all of Great Kerfuffle. But be that as it may, they were very definitely the bad guys, and as a result they spent an awful lot of time in jail.

They were in jail now, and—as if to prove how **evil** and **wicked** they truly were—they'd started the story without us.

'Hur hur hur,' laughed Rolf the Badger, a big badger with a big badge that said ⟨Big Badger⟩.

'What does hur hur hur mean?' asked Stewart the Badger, the smallest of the badgers.

'It's an **evil** and **wicked** laugh,' explained Rolf the Badger, showing him a big book entitled *The Big Book of **Evil** and **Wicked** Laughs.* 'I've been practising.'

'Never mind that,' said Harry the Badger, taking a sip of tea from a mug marked [World's Best Badger]. 'What do you think of my **evil** and **wicked** plan what I told you about just before the start of the story?'

'Oh, yeah!' said Rolf the Badger excitedly. 'I knew there was a reason I was doing my **evil** and **wicked** laugh! Yeah, it was a really, really **evil** and **wicked** plan. Wasn't it, badgers?'

'Yeah!' agreed the other badgers. 'Really **evil** and **wicked**. Let's do it!'

'But . . . ' said Stewart the Badger hesitantly, 'aren't we still in prison?'

The other badgers looked around. They were in a grey cell with a locked iron door, and bars on the windows, and a big sign on the wall saying:

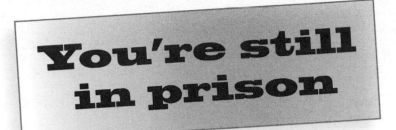

You're still in prison

'Oh, yeah,' they said gloomily. 'Bother. We can't do the **evil** and **wicked** plan if we're still in prison.'

'Maybe not,' said Harry the Badger. 'But I've also got a cunning plan, to go with the **evil** and **wicked** one. Do you remember those biscuits the army gave us last week?'

'Yeah,' said Rolf the Badger gloomily. 'They were horrible. All stale and dry and hard. I threw mine away.'

'Well, I didn't,' said Harry the Badger, his eyes narrowing craftily. 'I kept mine. And I've been scraping away at it with my teeth ever since . . .'

He held out his paw; and the badgers gasped, for in that paw lay a biscuit that had been cunningly nibbled into the shape of a key.

'Now,' said Harry the Badger, 'who's for that **evil** and **wicked** plan?'

said all the badgers excitedly; and they passed round *The Big Book of* **Evil** *and* **Wicked** *Laughs*, and each of them picked an **evil** and **wicked** laugh, and they laughed them all at the same time.

The effect was quite chilling.

chapter 2

In which our heroes awaken to face a day filled with adventures, much as a sandwich is filled with cheese[1]

It was morning. A warm breeze was blowing in from the sea, bringing with it the fresh ocean smells of salty water and sailors' socks. Cottony clouds drifted overhead; high above, the sun shone down, bright and kind; in the meadows, rabbits playfully fired one another out of catapults.

And in a tall tree in the garden of a lovely house high on a hillside above the tiny village of Loose Chippings, a blackbird was sitting on an air horn.

---

[1] Obviously, that would be a cheese sandwich. If it was a cucumber sandwich it would be filled with cucumber. And if it was a Victoria sandwich it would be filled with ~~Victoria~~ jam. But you get the idea.

'Paaaa

aaaaaaaaaaaaaaaaaaa

aaaaaaaaarrrrrrrp!'

went the air horn.

Inside the lovely house, in a beautiful pink bedroom, a little girl called Ketchup-Face leapt furiously out of bed. Racing to the window, she took aim with an enormous water-gun, and squeezed the trigger. With a noise somewhere between a **splooshhh!!!** and a **bang!!!**—a sort of

Splab
shhhh
hhhhh

oong
hhhhh
hh!!!!!

—the tank of the water-gun exploded, soaking
Ketchup-Face from head to toe and back again.

Drippingly, Ketchup-Face peered at the nozzle. It had been tightly bunged up with what looked suspiciously like blackbird feathers and chewed worms.

'Grrrr!'

grrrred Ketchup-Face grumpily, shaking her fist and a lot of water in the direction of the blackbird, which blew a **raspberry** and flew away.

Ketchup-Face stomped across the landing to her brother's bedroom and dried herself on his pyjamas. 'Come on, Stinkbomb,' she said. 'Time to get up.'

Stinkbomb got up wetly and looked at the clock. 'Gosh,' he said, wringing himself out. '**Chapter Two** already! We'd better get dressed and get on with the story.'

And they did.

Or, at least, they got dressed. After a bit, Ketchup-Face said, 'So what now?'

Stinkbomb shrugged. 'Now,' he said, 'we wait for the story to get here, I suppose. There'll probably be a knock on the door, or something.'

chapter 3

In which our heroes wait for the story to get here

Just then, there wasn't a knock on the door.
So they waited.

Chapter 4

In which the story still hasn't arrived

They waited some more.

After a bit, Ketchup-Face looked at the clock. **'Chapter Four!'** she said. 'And nothing's happened!'

'To us, anyway,' said Stinkbomb.

'What do you mean?' Ketchup-Face asked.

'Well,' Stinkbomb said, 'something must have happened to someone, somewhere in the story, or everyone would have stopped reading by now.'

'Stinkbomb!' Ketchup-Face exclaimed, struck by a horrible thought. 'What if we're not in the story. What if we just end up sitting here, doing nothing, while everyone else has all the adventures!'

'That wouldn't happen,' said Stinkbomb. 'I mean, we're the main characters. Our name's in all the titles and everything—

Stinkbomb & Ketchup-Face and the Badness of Badgers;

Stinkbomb & Ketchup-Face and the Quest for the Magic Porcupine;

Stinkbomb & Ketchup-Face
and the Evilness of Pizza...'

'But what if our name *isn't* in the title of this one!'
Ketchup-Face said, her tone horrified. 'What if
this one's called

Malcolm the Cat
and the Submarine of Treacle;

or

King Toothbrush Weasel
and the Exploding Sausage;

or

Stewart the Badger
& Rolf the Badger
& Harry the Badger
& All the Other
Badgers
and the **Terribly Bad
Thing That I Can't
Think Of Right Now!**'

'Gosh,' said Stinkbomb worriedly. 'I never thought of that. Well, if the story hasn't come to us, maybe we should go looking for the story!'

'Good idea!' said Ketchup-Face.

And off they set.

    🐀   🐀   🐀

It was a truly beautiful day. The sun was bright; all of nature was at play, and from everywhere came the sounds of animals glad to be alive. Across the fields towards them, **bleating** and **baa-ing** happily and gambolling for sheer joy, came a lovely fleecy flock of white woolly rats. In the stream, **quacking** away merrily, a proud mother rat swam, her brood of rats **cheeping** as they splashed along behind her. There was a flash of blue as a brightly coloured rat dived into the water and carried off a

rat in its beak, silver scales shining in the sunlight.
And high in the treetops, the rats **twittered** and
tweeted until it seemed as if the whole sky was
filled with ratsong.

`Um . . .
does some-
thing seem
a bit odd to
you?'

asked Stinkbomb.

'How do you mean?' his sister replied.

'Well . . . have you noticed that all these animals are rats dressed up?'

Ketchup-Face looked around carefully. 'So they are!' she said at last. 'I wonder why?'

'Er, yeah, sorry about that,' said a passing rat. 'It's just that, um, the author only just decided to put this scene in the story.'

'Oh, good,' said Stinkbomb relieved. 'We're definitely in the story, then.'

'Of course!' said the rat. 'You were supposed to go straight from your house to Loose Chippings, but then he thought that it would be nice to have a bit of description and stuff. But all the animals that he wanted to put in were busy doing their homework, and their mums and dads wouldn't let them come till they'd finished. So he had to use rats instead.'

'Oh,' said Ketchup-Face. 'Didn't *you* have any homework?'

'Oh, yeah,' said the rat. 'Lots. But we've already finished it. Contrary to popular belief, rats are very well-behaved and hard-working. Anyway, where was I? Oh, yeah: **sssssss**.'

And, hissing loudly, it slithered off into the undergrowth.

Stinkbomb and Ketchup-Face looked at each other, shrugged, and walked on through a lush meadow where trees blossomed, and wildflowers grew tall, and the air was filled with the gentle humming of rats as they **buzzed** gently from bloom to bloom, collecting nectar and pollen.

Soon they came to the tiny village of Loose Chippings. But—they could see immediately— something was wrong.

'Look!' Ketchup-Face cried dramatically. 'There's broken glass all over the street!'

'Yes,' said Stinkbomb, 'just in front of the sports shop!'

They rushed to investigate. Sure enough, the window of the *Great Kerfuffle Sporting Goods*

Emporium had been smashed to smithereens. Peering inside, they could see that one of the clothing racks had been emptied completely; only the hangers remained.

'Do you know what this means?' said Stinkbomb.

'Yes!' said Ketchup-Face.

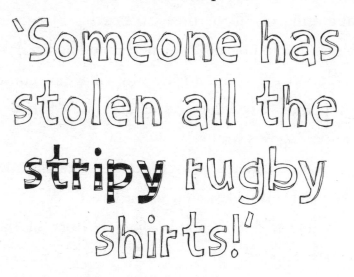

'Someone has stolen all the stripy rugby shirts!'

'And, look!' said Stinkbomb, turning and pointing. Across the street, another window had been smashed. This was the window of the *Great Kerfuffle Toy Shop*, and from where they stood, they could see that the dressing-up display that had been in the window only the day before had been ransacked.

'Do you know what this means?' said Stinkbomb.

'Yes!' said Ketchup-Face.

'Someone has stolen all the dressing-up fairy wings!'

'And, look!' said Stinkbomb, turning and pointing again at a sight that was enough to chill the blood of anyone who lived in Great Kerfuffle.

Ketchup-Face stared in horror. The door of the village jail was standing open. The jail itself was completely empty.

'Do you know what this means?' said Stinkbomb.

'Yes!' said Ketchup-Face.

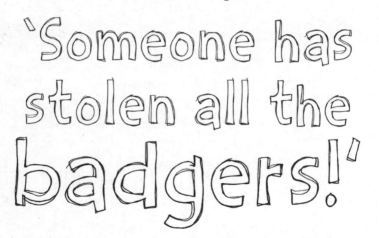

'Someone has stolen all the badgers!'

chapter 5

In which they go to see the king

They were still staring at the scene when they became aware of a trundling noise behind them, and, turning, they saw a welcome sight. It was their friend the little shopping trolley.

'Starlight!' said Ketchup-Face delightedly. 'My horsey!' She was, of course, talking about the little shopping trolley, which was not a horsey and which was not called Starlight. But Ketchup-Face was not the sort of child to whom details like that were important.

'Um, hello,' said the little shopping trolley shyly. 'What's going on?'

'Someone has stolen all the **stripy** rugby shirts and all the fairy wings and all the badgers!'

said Ketchup-Face excitedly.

'Really?' said the little shopping trolley doubtfully. 'Are you sure?'

'Oh, yes,' said Ketchup-Face firmly. 'Let's go and
tell King Toothbrush Weasel.' And she scrambled

into the little shopping trolley's basket. 'Come on, Stinkbomb!'

Stinkbomb shrugged. 'Might as well,' he said, climbing in after her.

'Giddy-up, Starlight!'

said Ketchup-Face.

'Um . . . ' said the little shopping trolley uncertainly, and then it shrugged too, and began to trundle.

The ride in the little shopping trolley was one of Ketchup-Face's favourite parts of any story, and she was always disappointed when the story skipped over it.

`Awwwww!'

she said, as they drew up outside King Toothbrush Weasel's palace. 'Can we do it again?'

'Sorry,' said Stinkbomb. 'We need to get on with the next bit now.'

You won't have seen a palace quite as small as King Toothbrush Weasel's. It was about the size of a small cottage, and had pretty little towers with thatched turrets, and dinky little battlements. It also had the sweetest little sentry box you've ever seen; and in front of the sentry box was the entire army of Great Kerfuffle, who was a small cat called Malcolm the Cat.

'Not you two again,' yawned Malcolm the Cat lazily, as Stinkbomb and Ketchup-Face hopped out of the little shopping trolley's basket.

'Yes!' Ketchup-Face said dramatically. 'It *is* us two again! And we have come to see King Tooth-brush Weasel!'

'Well, you can't,' said Malcolm the Cat.

'Oh,' said Ketchup-Face. 'OK. Come on, Stink-bomb.' And she clambered back into the little shopping trolley's basket.

'Or maybe ... ' said Malcolm the Cat thought-fully. 'No, maybe you can see him after all.'

'Great!' said Ketchup-Face, leaping out of the basket again.

'Oh, hang on. Sorry. You can't,' said Malcolm the Cat.

'Awww,' said Ketchup-Face, and scrambled back into the basket.

'Wait a minute,' said Malcolm the Cat. 'What day is it?'

Ketchup-Face scratched her head and thought for a bit. 'Ummm . . . . It's today,' she said at last.

'Oh, is it?' said Malcolm the Cat. 'I thought it was tomorrow. That's different. If it's today then you can definitely see him.'

'Oh, good,' said Ketchup-Face, jumping out of the basket.

'Oh, no, sorry,' said Malcolm the Cat. '*I* meant *yesterday*. You could see him if it was *yesterday*. Not today.'

'Bother,' said Ketchup-Face, getting back into the basket.

'Oh, wait,' said Malcolm the Cat. '*Did* I mean yesterday? No, silly me, *I did* mean today. Yes, you can see him.'

'Goody!' said Ketchup-Face, jumping out of the basket again.

'Unless we're in a story,' said Malcolm the Cat.

'Oh,' said Ketchup-Face, climbing back into the basket.

'Unless the story has got something to do with badgers,' added Malcolm the Cat.

There was no telling how long this could have gone on for, if Stinkbomb hadn't gently nudged the little shopping trolley forward a little just as Ketchup-Face was leaping out of the basket again.

'Ow!' said Malcolm the Cat.

'Oh, sorry,' said Ketchup-Face, looking down and taking her foot off Malcolm the Cat's tail.

And just at that moment, King Toothbrush Weasel came round the corner of the palace. He was dressed in a baggy white one-piece outfit, with white gloves and white boots and a little badge.

On his head was a very broad-brimmed hat from which a mesh veil hung down, covering his face and firmly attaching to his collar.

'Hello, King Toothbrush Weasel!' said Ketchup-Face cheerily.

King Toothbrush Weasel looked sternly at her. 'I am not King Toothbrush Weasel,' he said. 'I am the Royal Beekeeper.' He pointed to his badge, which said (Royal Beekeeper)

'Oh,' said Ketchup-Face. 'I didn't know there was a Royal Beekeeper.'

'Well, there is,' said King Toothbrush Weasel firmly. 'It's a very important job, because bees are so very important.'

'That's true,' said Stinkbomb. 'Bees are really important because they help so many crops and other plants to grow.'

'And they make honey!' added Ketchup-Face, pointing to a bit of honey on her cheek that was left over from yesterday's breakfast.

'Oh, do they?' said King Toothbrush Weasel. 'I thought they were just important because they make a nice noise.'

'You wouldn't keep bees just because they make a nice noise!' said Stinkbomb. 'It's not worth the risk of getting stung!'

'Bees don't sting!' retorted King Toothbrush Weasel.

'Of course they do!' said Stinkbomb. 'That's why you're wearing that outfit!'

'Is it?' said King Toothbrush Weasel. 'I thought this was just what beekeepers wore. You know, like the army wears a red jacket.'

'How many bees do you have?' Ketchup-Face asked.

'Four,' said King Toothbrush Weasel. 'Jessica, Ralph, Edward, and Susan.'

'*Four?*' said Stinkbomb. He was beginning to have suspicions about the royal bees. 'Um ... could we have a look at them?'

King Toothbrush Weasel led them round to the back of the palace where, just next to the dust-bin, they saw a large beehive.

'Well ... ' said Stinkbomb doubtfully. 'It certainly *looks* like a proper beehive ...'

'Of *course* it's a proper beehive,' said King Toothbrush Weasel indignantly. 'A proper beehive for proper bees. You don't get bees more properly beeish than my bees. My bees are the most properly beeish and bee-like bees in all of beeishness!'

And just at that moment, one of the bees stuck its head out of the beehive and said,

'Quack!'

chapter 6

In which they tell the king about the badgers

It took them quite some time to persuade the king that apparently he was not the Royal Beekeeper after all, but was in fact the Royal Duckkeeper, and that he had been keeping the ducks all wrong. Eventually Stinkbomb had to show him a book that he found in his pocket, which was called *How To Tell the Difference Between a Bee and a Duck*.

'Bother,' said King Toothbrush Weasel eventually. 'I'll have to go and find some bees now. How does a beekeeper find some bees to keep?'

'Um, I *think*,' said Stinkbomb, 'that you need to find some bees that are swarming.'

'But that isn't what we came to talk to you about, anyway!' interrupted Ketchup-Face.

'You came to talk to *me*?' said King Toothbrush Weasel, tapping the badge that said (Royal Beekeeper) .

'Er, no,' said Stinkbomb tactfully, 'she means we came to talk to the king.'

'But he is the OW!' said Ketchup-Face, as Stinkbomb elbowed her in the ribs. 'What did you do that for? I only said he was the OW! And he is the OW!'

'I am not the OW,' said King Toothbrush Weasel sternly. 'I am the Royal Beekeeper. However, I think I have just spotted His Royal Majesty King Toothbrush Weasel standing behind this tree, and if you wait here I shall go and fetch him.'

And with that, he stepped behind the tree, took off his beekeeping overalls, put on a small crown and a badge that said (King), and came out again.

'Ah, Stinkbomb and Ketchup-Face!' he said regally. 'What a pleasant surprise! What can I do for you?'

'Someone has stolen all the stripy rugby shirts

and all the fairy wings and all the badgers!'

Ketchup-Face told him excitedly.

'How peculiar,' said King Toothbrush Weasel, putting on his long golden beard and stroking it thoughtfully. 'There must be a gang of international fairy rugby badger thieves in the area. I shall tell the army to be on the lookout.'

'But we have to find them!' insisted Ketchup-Face. 'We can't leave our badgers all stolen!'

'Why not?' asked Stinkbomb.

Ketchup-Face thought about this. 'Well,' she said eventually, 'whoever stole the badgers is probably even more **evil** and **wicked** than the badgers!'

'Good point,' Stinkbomb agreed. 'They've probably stolen the badgers as part of some **evil** and **wicked** plan! And if we find the badgers, then we can find the **evil** and **wicked** badger thieves before they do their **evil** and **wicked** plan, and stop them doing it!'

'Yes,' said Ketchup-Face. 'But how are we going to find them?'

'Ah,' said King Toothbrush Weasel. 'I think I may have the answer to that. This leaflet came through the door the other day.'

He passed them a leaflet. It read:

Badger trouble?

Call the experts!

If badgers are bothering you, send for Ziggy and Wiggo! Brave, fearless, and from a long line of expert badger-hunters, their instinctive understanding of the furry fiends will make you gasp in admiration. So whether you want to find badgers or get rid of them . . .

Call Ziggy & Wiggo!

'Hurrah!' said Ketchup-Face. 'Let's go and call Ziggy and Wiggo!'

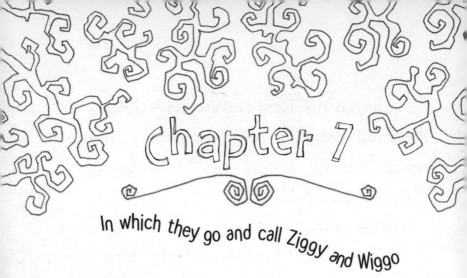

chapter 7

In which they go and call Ziggy and Wiggo

King Toothbrush Weasel led them into the palace and they called Ziggy and Wiggo.

Specifically, King Toothbrush Weasel called Ziggy and Wiggo, while Stinkbomb played with a football he'd found in his pocket and Ketchup-Face pretended to sing a song.

It wasn't a very long phone call.

'Excellent,' said King Toothbrush Weasel, putting the phone down. 'Ziggy and Wiggo said they'd be round straight away.'

Just then, there was a knock on the door.

'Excellent,' said King Toothbrush Weasel again. 'That will be them now. Answer the door, will you, Ketchup-Face?'

Ketchup-Face went to the door and opened it. For a moment, there was nobody there; and then an excited voice yapped, 'Badger!' and

suddenly Ketchup-Face was on her back in the hallway with two small dogs sitting on her chest and yelping

'Badger!
Badger!
Badger!
Badger!'

'I'm not a badger!' Ketchup-Face said indignantly.

'Aren't you?' said the bigger dog.

'Are you *sure*?' asked the smaller suspiciously.

Ketchup-Face sat up, and the two dogs fell off and landed on their backs on the floor.

'Of *course* I'm sure,' she said. 'I'm a little girl! I'd *know* if I was a badger!'

'Ah, but *would* you?' asked the bigger one, still lying on its back.

'While I'm down here,' added the smaller, 'you don't fancy tickling my tummy, do you?'

'Anyway,' the bigger one went on, 'if you're a little girl, where are your parents?'

Ketchup-Face shrugged. 'Don't know,' she said. 'They like to stay out of the way while we're in a story.'

The dogs rolled onto their feet. 'Oooh!' the bigger one said. 'Are we in a story?' The smaller one just yipped excitedly and did a funny little half-jump with his front legs.

King Toothbrush Weasel stepped into the hallway. 'Ah,' he began. 'You must be Ziggy and Wiggo ...'

'Badger!'

yelped the smaller one, and suddenly King Toothbrush Weasel was on his back in the hallway with two small dogs tearing his ceremonial beard off.

'I say!' King Toothbrush Weasel said. 'What are you doing?'

'It's a badger,' explained the bigger dog, shaking the beard enthusiastically.

'No it isn't,' said King Toothbrush Weasel crossly, grabbing the beard back and accidentally putting it on upside down. It stuck straight up from the top of his head, dropping little droplets of doggy-dribble onto his nose. 'It's my royal beard. And I am King Toothbrush Weasel.'

'Ah,' said the bigger dog. 'Hello, your royalness. I'm Ziggy, and this is Wiggo.'

Just then, there was a loud crash from the throne room. They rushed in to see Stinkbomb standing with an embarrassed look on his face, and indeed all over his body. There was also a broken vase on the floor, and a football on the royal coffee table.

yelped Wiggo, and he and Ziggy jumped on the football and punctured it with their teeth.

'That's not a badger!' said Stinkbomb. 'It's my football!'

'No it isn't,' said Ziggy. 'Footballs are round.'

'*My* football was round until you burst it!' said Stinkbomb.

'Oh,' said Ziggy.

'Anyway,' said Wiggo, 'which one of you is the badger?'

Ketchup-Face rolled her eyes. 'None of us is badgers, you sillies!' she said. 'We don't even know where the badgers *are*!'

'Ah-hah!' said Wiggo, leaping **up** and **down** and wagging his tail excitedly. 'Well, we can help you there! We're badger experts!'

'I don't think you are, actually,' said Stink-bomb. 'You don't seem to know what a badger is.'

'Ah. Yes. Well,' said Ziggy. 'The thing is, we've never actually *seen* a badger.'

'But when we see one, we'll know what it is!' added Wiggo.

'Prove it!' said Ketchup-Face.

'Easy,' said Ziggy. 'We're dachshunds. And *dachshund* is German for *badger-dog*. So we must be experts.'

'Yeah,' Wiggo agreed. 'That's what dachshunds are *for*. Catching badgers.'

'Well, that's good enough for me,' said King Toothbrush Weasel happily. 'Let's go and find some badgers.'

chapter 8

In which they go to find some badgers

Fortunately, the little shopping trolley had waited outside for them.

Ziggy and Wiggo leapt straight into the basket with a yelp of `Badger!' and tried to wrestle it to the ground. Ketchup-Face had to explain to them that it was not a badger, but was in fact a horsey; and then the little shopping trolley had to explain that it was not a horsey, but was in fact a little shopping trolley; and then everybody else got in and off they trundled. Ziggy complained a bit because Malcolm the Cat got in on top of him; but Malcolm the Cat just yawned and said, 'Hmmmm. It's comfier than usual.'

Ketchup-Face, meanwhile, picked up Wiggo and cuddled him. She had always wanted a pet of her own, and was unwilling to let this opportunity pass.

It wasn't long before they spotted some creatures wandering along by the side of the road.

'Oh, look!' said King Toothbrush Weasel. 'Llamas!' And they all climbed out of the little shopping trolley for a closer look, except for Malcolm the Cat, who couldn't be bothered, and Ziggy, who couldn't because of being under Malcolm the Cat.

'We're not llamas!' said one of the creatures indignantly. 'We're bees!'

'You're not bees!' said King Toothbrush
Weasel. 'You haven't said **quack** once!'

'No, you silly king,' said Ketchup-Face. 'That's
ducks. Remember?'

'Are you *sure* you're bees?' asked Stinkbomb,
who had learned over the course of the last
three books to be suspicious of this sort of conversation.

'Oh, yes,' said one of the bees earnestly. 'We're definitely bees. We're very beeish indeed. Isn't that right, Rolf the Bee?'

'That's right,' agreed Rolf the Bee, a big bee with a big badge that said (Big Bee). 'We're bees all right. Aren't we, Harry the Bee?'

'Yes,' agreed Harry the Bee, taking a sip of tea from a mug marked [World's Best Bee]. 'We're extremely beeish. Aren't we, Stewart the Bee?'

Just as Stewart the Bee was opening his mouth to answer, Harry the Bee passed him a note that said:

> Pretend we're bees.

Stewart the Bee read it slowly three times and then said, 'Er, we're bees.' He turned the note over. On the other side it said:

Don't let them know we're badgers.

'Er, we're not badgers,' he added.

Stinkbomb narrowed his eyes. 'How do we *know* you're bees?' he asked.

'Well,' said Harry the Bee, 'we're stripy, and we've got wings.'

Stinkbomb and Ketchup-Face looked at Harry the Bee. He was indeed stripy, and he did indeed have wings. Pink ones, with sequins on.

'And we're collecting nectar and pollen,' added Rolf the Bee. 'Look!' He showed them a big bucket he was carrying. It was full of flowers.

'Um . . . I think you're supposed to take the nectar and pollen *out* of the flowers, aren't you?' Stinkbomb asked.

'It's much easier this way,' Rolf the Bee assured him, as Stewart the Bee threw some more flowers into the bucket.

'Wait a minute!' said King Toothbrush Weasel excitedly. 'Are you swarming?'

The bees looked at each other uncertainly. One or two of them **shuffled** their paws, and Stewart the Bee whispered to Rolf the Bee, 'Er . . . what's *swarming*?' Rolf the Bee put on a don't-know face and shrugged his shoulders.

Eventually, Harry the Bee said, 'Um . . . I suppose so,' and looked at King Toothbrush Weasel to see if it was the right answer.

King Toothbrush Weasel beamed. 'Excellent!' he said.

All the bees relaxed. 'Oh, yeah,' they said. 'We're swarming, all right.'

'That is good news,' said King Toothbrush Weasel happily. 'You see, I need . . . I mean, my Royal Beekeeper needs some bees to keep. You can't be a beekeeper unless you're keeping some bees. So, would you like to come and be *my* bees?'

'Depends,' said Harry the Bee cunningly. 'What's in it for us?'

'Well,' said King Toothbrush Weasel, 'you'd get to live in a lovely big beehive, just round the back of the palace.'

'Next to the dustbin,' added Ketchup-Face helpfully, still cuddling Wiggo.

said Wiggo suddenly, trying to wriggle out of Ketchup-Face's grasp.

'No, you silly,' said Ketchup-Face, cuddling him tighter. 'That's not a badger. It's a ladybird.'

'Yeah,' said the ladybird, crawling down Wiggo's nose to the end and then flying away.

'Oh,' said Wiggo, and settled down again. He was secretly rather enjoying being cuddled.

'We could move the dustbin somewhere else if it's a problem,' said King Toothbrush Weasel, suddenly worried that bees might not like the smell of dustbins.

'Oh, no,' said Harry the Bee quickly. 'We don't mind dustbins, do we, bees?'

All the other bees quickly shook their heads and said no, they didn't mind dustbins at all.

'Lovely!' said King Toothbrush Weasel. 'So what do you say?'

The bees put their heads together and muttered for a bit. It sounded very muttery, although occasionally you could hear something a bit more clearly, like 'dustbin', or 'palace', or 'beehive', or 'hur hur hur'.

'Excuse me,' said Stinkbomb. 'But did one of you just laugh an **evil** and **wicked** laugh?'

'Er, no,' said Rolf the Bee quickly. 'That wasn't an **evil** and **wicked** laugh. I just . . . er . . . I was just in the middle of **buzzing**, and I coughed. That's what *that* was.'

'Oh, OK,' said Stinkbomb.

'So,' said King Toothbrush Weasel, 'do we have a deal?'

'Er, yeah, all right,' said Harry the Bee. 'It'll probably be nicer than where we've come from.'

'And where would that be?' asked King Toothbrush Weasel politely. He wasn't really interested in where the bees had come from, but he'd read recently that this was the sort of thing kings were supposed to say when making conversation with their subjects, and he'd been looking for a chance to try it out.

'Er ...' said Harry the Bee.

'Um ...' said Rolf the Bee.

'We've just come from *MMMMMMM,*' explained Stewart the Bee, as Harry the Bee shoved something in his mouth.

'And where would that be?' asked King Tooth-brush Weasel politely.

Stewart the Bee reached into his mouth and pulled out the thing that Harry the Bee had just shoved in there. 'I didn't mean *MMMMMMM,*' he said, and looked at the thing. It was a note that said:

Don't tell them we've been in prison.

Stewart the Bee read it slowly three times and then said, 'Er, we haven't been in prison.' He turned the note over. On the other side it said:

Pretend we've come from somewhere else.

'Er, we've come from somewhere else,' he added.

'And where would that be?' asked King Toothbrush Weasel politely.

'Er . . . ' said Stewart the Bee, looking nervously around for help but finding none. 'Er . . . Somewhere else.'

'And where would that be?' asked King Toothbrush Weasel politely.

'Er . . . ' said Stewart the Bee again, checking in his mouth in case someone had put another helpful note in there when he wasn't looking.

'Stupidity!' said Rolf the Bee, suddenly remembering somewhere he'd once been. 'We've come from Stupidity!'

'And where would that be?' asked King Toothbrush Weasel politely.

'You remember, Your Majesty!' said Ketch-up-Face. 'It's the tiny village where the famous Magic Porcupine lives.'

'And where would that be?' asked King Tooth-brush Weasel politely. The conversation seemed to be going very well, in his opinion, and for a moment he wondered if he would need to say anything other than 'And where would that be?' ever again.

'Where would what be?' asked Stinkbomb, who had noticed that the conversation wasn't making much sense any more.

'I don't know,' admitted King Toothbrush Weasel. 'I wasn't really listening. What were you saying?' he added, looking at Harry the Bee.

'Er . . . I was saying that it'd be nicer than where we've just come from.'

'And where would that be?' asked King Toothbrush Weasel politely.

'They already told you, you silly king,' said Ketchup-Face. 'They've come from Stupidity.'

'And where would that be?' asked King Toothbrush Weasel politely.

'There it is,' said Stinkbomb, pulling a copy of **Stinkbomb & Ketchup-Face and the Quest for the Magic Porcupine** out of his pocket and pointing to Stupidity on the map at the front of the book. 'But right now, I think we'd better go and look for the badgers.'

All the bees sniggered.

'Yes,' agreed Ketchup-Face. 'We need to find the place where our poor badgers have been stolen to!'

'And where would that be?' asked King Toothbrush Weasel politely.

'Don't know,' said Ketchup-Face. 'But these bees

need to go back to your palace and get in the bee-hive. They'll have to move the ducks first.'

'Oh, yes,' said King Toothbrush Weasel. 'Off you go, then, bees. Make yourselves at home, and my Royal Beekeeper will attend to you when we get back.'

'We'll make ourselves at home, all right,' said Rolf the Bee, and all the other bees sniggered again.

'And now we'd better **buzz** off,' said Harry the Bee.

'Buzz off!' said the other bees, and they all laughed as though Harry the Bee had made a really funny joke, even though it was actually a bit rubbish; and then they went and stood at a nearby bus stop.

'Funny,' said Stinkbomb. 'I didn't think bees travelled by bus.'

'Badger!'

yelped Wiggo, wriggling.

'Er, no,' said the little shopping trolley. 'That's the **number 47** bus.'

chapter 9

In which they run into trouble

They watched as the bees boarded the bus, and the bus pulled away.

'So,' said the little shopping trolley hesitantly, as they all climbed back into its basket, 'which way shall we go?'

Ziggy and Wiggo sat up—at least, as much as two small dogs can sit up when one is being cuddled by a little girl and the other is being sat on by the army—and **sniffed** the air.

'*That* way!' they both said in very definite voices, pointing with their noses.

Unfortunately, they were each pointing in a different direction.

'Are you *sure* you're experts in finding badgers?' Stinkbomb asked.

'Oh, yes,' said Ziggy.

'Um . . . could someone get this cat off me, please?'

Malcolm the Cat gave a loud snore.

'We can't move him now,' said Ketchup-Face. 'It wouldn't be kind. He's asleep.'

'I don't think he really *is* asleep,' said Stink-bomb.

'Yes, I am!' said Malcolm the Cat indignantly.

'Oh, OK,' said Stinkbomb. 'Sorry. I thought you were only pretending to be asleep.'

'Well, I'm not,' said Malcolm the Cat. 'I really am asleep, and if you don't stop talking to me you're going to wake me up, and that would be unkind.'

'Sorry,' said Stinkbomb again.

'Hmmph,' said Malcolm the Cat crossly. 'Well, don't do it again.' And he gave another loud snore.

'Sorry, Ziggy,' said Ketchup-Face. 'Looks like you're stuck there until Malcolm the Cat wakes up.'

'Shall we get on?' interrupted King Tooth-brush Weasel. 'If our badger experts can't decide, then I vote we go that way.' He pointed. 'And since I'm the king, my vote wins. Off we go!'

'Yes, Your Majesty,' said the little shopping trolley; and off they went.

Soon they were **galloping**—in a squeaky-wheeled sort of way—along a narrow road across a wild and desolate heath. On either side of them dark forbidding hills rose up, and ahead of them a great mountain range loomed threateningly.

'This seems to be a bit of my kingdom I've never actually visited before,' mused King Tooth-brush Weasel. 'I wonder where we are?'

'Let me see,' said Stinkbomb, pulling out his copy of

Stinkbomb & Ketchup-Face
and the Quest for the
Magic Porcupine

and looking at the map again. 'Do those mountains look a bit **doomy** to you?'

Everybody looked at the mountains and agreed that, yes, they did look sort of **doomy**, now that Stinkbomb mentioned it.

'And does this valley look sort of **despairy**?'

Everybody looked around the valley and agreed that, yes, **despairy** was quite a good word for it.

'Ah,' said Stinkbomb. 'Then I expect those are the Mountains of **Doom**. And this is probably the Valley of **Despair**.'

'Isn't that a terrible, desolate place filled with deadly kittens?' asked King Toothbrush Weasel worriedly.

'No, your majesty,' said Stinkbomb, flicking to **page 58** to check. 'Deadly *snakes*.'

'I don't see any deadly snakes,'

said Ketchup-Face.

'They're probably lying in wait for us,' said Stinkbomb darkly.

'*Look out!*' said Miss Butterworth the ninja librarian, in a voice like the tinkling of wind-chimes.

'Miss Butterworth!' said Ketchup-Face in delight and astonishment.

'How did *you* get here?' asked Stinkbomb, equally pleased and surprised.

'Ow,' said Malcolm the Cat.

'*Oh, sorry,*' said Miss Butterworth, looking down and taking her foot off Malcolm the Cat's tail. Then she wriggled sideways a bit, the way that people do when they're sitting in a little shopping trolley with too many other people, and said, *'Now, where was I? Oh, yes: Look out!'*

At her warning, the little shopping trolley screeched to a halt, and the travellers looked to see what was wrong. As they did, a group of menacing shapes emerged from the cover of a large and prickly gorse bush ahead of them.

'Wh-who are *they*?' asked Ketchup-Face anxiously.

Miss Butterworth was dressed all in black from head to toe; only her wise, kind eyes were visible, behind her sensible glasses. So it was difficult to tell whether she had actually turned pale, but she certainly *sounded* pale as she whispered, *'Of all the terrors the world has to offer, this is one I had hoped never to encounter!'*

The little shopping trolley, meanwhile, had begun to shake violently. 'Oh, dear,' it muttered to itself. 'Oh, dear, oh, dear, oh, dear.'

'Yes?' said a roe deer; and then, noticing the approaching figures, it went, `Eeek!' and ran away.

'Villains!' said King Toothbrush Weasel dramatically, standing up in the little shopping trolley and pointing at the sinister newcomers. 'Whoops!' he added, losing his balance and sitting down with a bump.

`Badger!'

yelped Wiggo, wriggling wildly.

'They are not badgers,' said Miss Butterworth firmly.

'But who *are* they?' repeated Ketchup-Face, through a mouthful of wriggling dachshund.

'They are the most feared bandits ever to roam the kingdom of Great Kerfuffle,' Miss Butterworth said

grimly. *'According to legend, after years of enslavement they turned on their former masters and there was a most horrible battle. But though they won their freedom, the years of cruelty had done untold damage. Vowing their revenge on the entire world, they became the dreadful bandits you now see before you.'*

"'Tis true!' snarled one of the bandits savagely. 'Our former masters were the cruellest beings imaginable!'

'Who were they?' Stinkbomb asked curiously. 'And what did they do to you? I mean—it can't have been *that* bad, can it?'

'It was worse!'

roared the bandit. 'Our masters were the barbarous firm of accountants known as . . . A.C. Bartlett & Sons Ltd!'

roared the other bandits furiously.

'And as for what they did,' the first bandit went on, 'they used to . . . they used to . . . '

'Yes?' Stinkbomb asked.

'They used to *sit on us!*' shrieked the bandit, and all the other bandits **howled** and **jabbered** like souls in torment. 'In their offices!'

'Oh,' said Stinkbomb. 'I mean . . . well . . . that certainly doesn't sound very nice. I don't think I'd like it. But after all, you are . . . Well, you're office chairs, aren't you? I mean, if you're office chairs, people are going to put you in offices and sit on you, aren't they?'

There was a dreadful silence, broken only by Miss Butterworth's whispered, *'I don't think you should have said that.'*

One of the chairs—clearly the leader—trundled forward on its little wheels and fixed Stinkbomb with what would have been a most terrible stare, if only chairs had eyes to stare with.

'But it's true, isn't it?' persisted Stinkbomb. 'I mean—I'm not being rude, but you really *are* office chairs.'

The bandit leader—a large, imposing executive chair with a luxuriously padded leather seat, a smooth, silent swivel action, and a patented *Fastglide*™ power-assisted hydraulic up-and-down seat mechanism—growled softly. 'Fifteen years,' it said, in a tone of utter menace. 'Fifteen years I laboured under an accountant's bottom. Fifteen years of sweat—none of it my own. Fifteen years of pain and toil and nasty smells. And for fifteen years I swore that if I escaped and won my freedom, no one would ever again call me an office chair and escape unpunished.'

'Aaaaargh,'

agreed the other chairs, rolling threateningly forward, their little wheels **rattling** and **squeaking** angrily.

'Wait!' commanded King Toothbrush Weasel, standing regally but rather more carefully. 'Before you attack us, know this—I am His Royal Highness King Toothbrush Weasel, ruler of the Kingdom and Dominions of Great Kerfuffle, even unto the little crinkly bits round the edge!'

'So?' asked the bandit leader rudely; and all the other chairs sniggered and made mocking noises.

'Er . . . just thought you ought to know,' said King Toothbrush Weasel feebly, and sat down again. 'Oh—wait. I remember!' he continued, standing up once more. 'So if you attack my royal carriage, know this—I am guarded by the entire army!'

'Miaow,' added the army lazily, licking its paw and cleaning behind its ear. Then it remembered it was asleep, and snored loudly; but not before Ziggy had taken the opportunity to wriggle out from underneath it and give himself a good shake.

'I'm not afraid of the army!' said the bandit leader defiantly.

'Anyway,' added one of the other chairs, 'it's just a cat.'

'Oh, is it?' said the bandit leader. 'I am a bit scared of cats, to be honest. But only a bit. Not enough to stop us attacking you and subjecting you to the most fearsome punishment known to furniturekind!'

'What are you going to do to us?' demanded Ketchup-Face.

'We're going to spin you round really fast,' **hissed** the leader, 'until you go all dizzy and can't stand up and feel a bit sick. Grab them!'

chapter 10

In which the office chairs attack

The office chairs howled in triumphant fury. It was a bloodcurdling sound.

'Stinkbomb,' whispered Ketchup-Face, 'I think my blood's just **curdled**.'

Stinkbomb thought for a moment. 'I don't think it actually does that,' he said. 'It's just a saying.'

'Oh,' said Ketchup-Face. 'Good. What *is* **curdling**, anyway?'

'Well,' said Stinkbomb, 'I'm not exactly sure, but I think it means like when milk goes all lumpy and . . .'

'Excuse me,' interrupted the bandit leader impatiently, 'but can we get on? We're meant to be attacking you, and we can't do it properly if you're just standing there having a conversation about **curdling** or whatever.'

'Oh, sorry,' said Stinkbomb.

'Right,' said the bandit leader. 'Where were we?'

'Um . . . we'd just got to the bit about the bloodcurdling howl,' said one of the other chairs, a cheap vinyl-covered model with a plastic frame and a loose headrest.

'Oh, yes, so we had,' said the bandit leader, and once more the office chairs howled in triumphant fury. It was a **bloodcurdling** sound.

At this Miss Butterworth, in a single fluid movement, rose to her feet and leapt from the shopping trolley, somersaulting twice in the air

before landing with the grace of a panther, hands upraised and feet apart in a fighting stance.

'STOP!'

she commanded.

The leader swivelled to face her. 'Who are you?' it growled.

'*I*,' said Miss Butterworth, '*am Miss Butterworth of the Ancient Order of Ninja Librarians. And this,*' she added, drawing her big sword, '*is my big sword.*'

said all the office chairs, impressed.

'*Quickly!*' Miss Butterworth said quietly to the little shopping trolley. '*When they attack me, flee! As fast as you can, get the children to safety!*'

'Miss Butterworth!' Ketchup-Face said in alarm. 'No!'

'*Go!*' Miss Butterworth insisted. '*Don't worry about me!*'

'I'm not sure I can do that,' said Ketchup-Face. 'I mean, if you're worried about someone, you're worried about them, aren't you? I can't just not be worried about you, just because you say *Don't worry about me*, can I? It's like if you're hungry and someone says *Don't be hungry*. You're still hungry.'

'Yes,' agreed Stinkbomb. 'Or if you're not even slightly sleepy and someone says *Go to sleep*. Or if you can't think of anything to do and a grown-up says *Well, just think of something to do*. Or if . . . '

'Hey!' snapped the bandit leader. 'You're doing it again! Honestly, anybody would think you didn't want us to attack you and subject you to the most fearsome punishment known to furniturekind!'

Stinkbomb thought about this. The idea of being attacked and subjected to the most fearsome punishment known to furniturekind certainly sounded interesting, but on balance he wasn't sure if he fancied it. So he said, 'Er, well, we don't, actually.'

'Oh,' said the bandit leader. 'Well, fair enough, I suppose. But we're still going to. Get them!'

'*No!*' Miss Butterworth said, stepping forward. '*Anyone who wishes to attack these children must face my big sword!*'

'Then you'll be first!' the bandit leader snarled. 'Get her!'

And with another **bloodcurdling** howl, and much **rattling** and **squeaking** of little wheels, the office chairs hurled themselves at Miss Butterworth and fell down a hole in the ground.

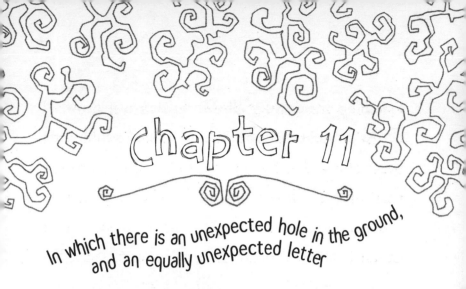

chapter 11

In which there is an unexpected hole in the ground, and an equally unexpected letter

Stinkbomb & Ketchup-Face leapt out of the little shopping trolley and ran to the hole in the ground.

'That was lucky, wasn't it?' said Ketchup-Face.

'Yes,'

said Miss Butterworth, peering into the hole with them.

'Indeed it was,' said King Toothbrush Weasel.

'It's a good thing all this heather was growing across the hole so they didn't see it!' said Stinkbomb.

'Badger!'

yelped Ziggy, pouncing on a tuft of heather and almost falling down the hole.

The hole was very deep, and full of office chairs.

'Um . . . excuse me,' said the bandit leader, 'but could you possibly help us out of this hole?'

'That depends,' said Stinkbomb. 'If we help you out of the hole, are you going to attack us and subject us to the most fearsome punishment known to furniturekind?'

The office chairs muttered together for a moment, and then the bandit leader looked up and said, 'Yes, probably. I expect we will. It certainly sounds like the sort of thing we'd do.'

'Oh,' said Stinkbomb. 'Well, in that case, I don't think we will help you get out.'

'Awwww!'

said the office chairs.

'Then we will have our revenge on you when we escape!' said the bandit leader defiantly.

'What sort of revenge?' Ketchup-Face asked.

'Um . . . the sort of revenge where we attack you and subject you to the most fearsome punishment known to furniturekind, probably,' said the bandit leader; and all the other office chairs howled and jabbered their agreement, with much fearsome rattling of little wheels.

'So . . .' said Stinkbomb slowly, 'if we help you

out of the hole, you'll attack us and subject us to the most fearsome punishment known to furniturekind; but if we don't help you out of the hole, you'll attack us and subject us to the most fearsome punishment known to furniturekind. Is that right?'

'Yep!' said the bandit leader cheerily; and then paused. 'Oh. Yes. I see what you mean. No, I probably wouldn't help us out of the hole either, in that case. OK, well, off you go and get on with the story. We'll see you later.'

'Are you definitely *in* the story later?' Ketchup-Face asked.

'Um . . . I'm not completely sure, to be honest,' the bandit leader said. 'But it'd be a shame if we weren't. I bet people have really enjoyed reading about us.'

'Oh, OK,' said Ketchup-Face. 'See you later.'

'Oh—before we go,' added Stinkbomb, 'you haven't stolen any badgers, have you?'

'Or rugby shirts or fairy wings?' added Ketchup-Face.

'Badgers? No,' said the bandit leader. 'Can't imagine why anyone would want to steal badgers.'

'The fairy wings sound fun, though,' added a badly-cushioned grey chair with an ink-stained seat. 'We ought to steal some of those one day.'

'OK,' said Stinkbomb. 'Bye, bandits.'

'Bye!' said all the office chairs; and then, thinking that maybe that didn't sound quite villainous enough, they added, 'Grrrrr!!!!!'

Stinkbomb, Ketchup-Face, King Toothbrush Weasel, and Miss Butterworth stepped back. As they did, there came from behind them a yelp of

'Badger!'

Turning, Stinkbomb and Ketchup-Face were horrified to see Ziggy and Wiggo hurling themselves at a deadly snake. The deadly snake reared up, raising its hooded head and displaying its lethal fangs, its little beadlike eyes glittering. Then Ziggy and Wiggo were upon it, and all was a blur of deadly snake and dachshund. Ketchup-Face squealed, not with fright but just because she felt that somebody ought to. The dogs and the serpent **twisted** like a tornado, **whirling** and **writhing**, **wrestling wildly**, **savagely spinning** as they fought furiously for the upper hand. Or paw. Or whatever it is deadly snakes have.

And then, suddenly, it was over. Ziggy and Wiggo, gripped in the deadly snake's savage coils,

stared in horror as the creature brought its poison-
ous fangs closer, closer, closer, and then opened its
mouth . . .

. . . and said, 'I am *not* a badger!'

'Oh, OK,' said Ziggy.

'The little girl's cuddles are nicer than yours,' added Wiggo.

'I'm not cuddling you!' the deadly snake protested. 'I'm just stopping you from fighting me while I deliver this message. Now—where did I drop it? Oh, there it is!'

It bent down, picked up a letter in its jaws, and handed it to Stinkbomb. 'Nice to see you two again, by the way,' it added. 'We've met before— in Stinkbomb & Ketchup-Face and the Quest for the Magic Porcupine. **Chapter Fifty**, I think it was.'

'Oh, yes!' said Ketchup-Face. 'At the bus-stop!'

'That's right!' agreed the deadly snake. 'Anyway, lovely to see you. Bye!'

And it uncoiled and slithered off, leaving

Stinkbomb and Ketchup-Face to read the letter, which said:

Dear characters,

I'm afraid the story has gone horribly wrong. Sorry about this, but you're not supposed to be in the Valley of Despair at all. You should be back at the Royal Palace. You need to get there by the beginning of the next **chapter**.

'What?' said the little shopping trolley. 'I'll never get us all there in time! It's too far! And I'm really tired!'

I expect the little shopping trolley will be too tired to get you there in time,

the letter continued,

so I've arranged for some extra-fast transport for you. Any second now, a magnificent carriage pulled by a team of twenty-four fleet-footed stallions driven by an expert coachman will arrive and whisk you back to the palace.

Just as they read this, there was a loud **whinnying** and a **thundering** of hooves.

That'll be them now.

The letter went on.

Off you go! No time to lose!

Everyone turned to see a wonderful sight. Coming towards them was a magnificent carriage pulled by a team of twenty-four fleet-footed rats driven by an expert coachrat.

Oh, sorry,

added the letter,

apparently the twenty-four fleet-footed stallions are still doing their homework, and the expert coachman has to help them with their spellings. But I'm sure the rats will do a wonderful job. Right, off you go! Remember, you've got to get back to the Royal Palace by the beginning of the next **chapter**.

Lots of love
The author xxx

Just as they finished reading, the magnificent carriage pulled up next to them.

`Badger!`

yelped Wiggo, and he and Ziggy were half-way through leaping at the coachrat when Stinkbomb and Ketchup-Face grabbed them and bundled them into the carriage. Everybody tumbled in after them—even the little shopping trolley, for the magnificent carriage was equipped with a magnificent ramp—and with a great **whinnying** and **stamping** of hooves, the twenty-four fleet-footed rats were off, **galloping** furiously towards the Royal Palace and the next **chapter**.

chapter 12

In which they arrive at the palace again,
and our heroes go round the back

Just in time for the beginning of the **chapter**, the magnificent carriage drew up outside King Toothbrush Weasel's palace.

'Not *again*,' grumbled Ketchup-Face. 'Why does the story keep skipping over the best bits?'

'No time for that now!' said Stinkbomb, leaping out of the magnificent carriage. 'We've got to . . . er . . . What *have* we got to do, now we're here?'

Everyone looked at each other.

'*I do not know,*' said Miss Butterworth after a moment. She closed her eyes and concentrated. '*There is a disturbance in the story, but I cannot tell what should happen next.*'

'We could sing a song,' suggested Ketchup-Face hopefully.

'I don't think that would help,' said the little shopping trolley hesitantly.

'Badger!'

yelped Wiggo, scrambling out of the carriage and throwing himself on a garden gnome.

'I wonder how the Royal Bees are getting on,' said King Toothbrush Weasel.

'Let's go round to the beehive,' suggested Stink-bomb.

'And where would that be?' asked King Tooth-brush Weasel politely.

'Round the back of the palace, you silly king,' said Ketchup-Face.

'And where would that be?' asked King Tooth-brush Weasel politely.

Stinkbomb and Ketchup-Face sighed, and led the way.

'That's odd,' said King Toothbrush Weasel, rounding the corner at the back of the palace. 'I wonder how the dustbin got knocked over.'

'And there's no sign of the bees!' said Stinkbomb. 'They definitely should have got here by now.'

'Maybe they're in the beehive?' suggested Ketchup-Face.

Just at that moment, a duck stuck its head out of the beehive and said, **'Quack!'**

'I wonder if the ducks have any idea where the bees might be?' said Stinkbomb.

'Let's ask them!' said Ketchup-Face.

'Um . . . I don't think any of us knows how to talk in duck language,' said King Toothbrush Weasel.

'I do!' Ketchup-Face said confidently, and she strode up to the duck and said, **'Quack!'**

The duck looked at her in some surprise, and replied, **'Quack! Quack quack quack!'**

'Quack?' said Ketchup-Face. **'Quack quack quack quack quack? Quack quack quack quack quack quack; quack quack quack, quack quack-quack quack quack quack-quack-quack, quack quack-quack quack quack.'**

'Quack!' the duck agreed. **'Quack quack quack quack quack, quack quack**

quack quack quack, quack quackity quack.'

'**Quack quack quack quack!**' said Ketchup-Face. '**Quack quack quack quack quack quack quack quack!**'

At this, the duck looked utterly astonished. It stroked its beak with its wing for a moment, and then suggested, '**Quaaaaack quack-quack quaaaaack quack-quack quack quack quack, quack quaaack quack quaaaaak quack quaaaack, quack quack-quack quack quack quack quaaaack quaaaack quaaaaaack quaaaaack, quack-quack quack quack quack quack quack, quack quack quack quack quack. Quack quack quack, quack quack quack, quack quack quack quack quack. Quack!**'

Ketchup-Face smiled. '**Quack** you very much,' she said, and returned to her brother and the king.

'What did it say?' asked Stinkbomb.

'Well,' said Ketchup-Face, 'first it said, **"Quack! Quack quack quack!"** and then **it said "Quack! Quack quack quack quack quack, quack quack quack quack quack, quack quackity quack"**, and then . . . '

'No,' Stinkbomb interrupted. 'I mean, what did all those **quacks** *mean*?'

Ketchup-Face shrugged. 'Dunno,' she said happily.

'But you said you knew how to speak duck language!' said King Toothbrush Weasel.

'I do,' Ketchup-Face said. 'I just don't know how to *understand* duck language.'

Stinkbomb sighed. 'Well, what did you *say* to the duck?'

'Oh, that's easy,' said Ketchup-Face. 'First, I said **"Quack!"** and then I said **"Quack? Quack quack quack quack quack? Quack quack quack quack quack quack; quack quack quack, quack quack-quack quack quack quack-quack-quack, quack quack-quack quack quack",** and then I said . . .'

'Oh, never mind,' said Stinkbomb. 'So how do we find out where the bees are?'

'We could ask that one,' said King Toothbrush Weasel, and he pointed to the bottom of the garden, where a bee was just coming through the gate.

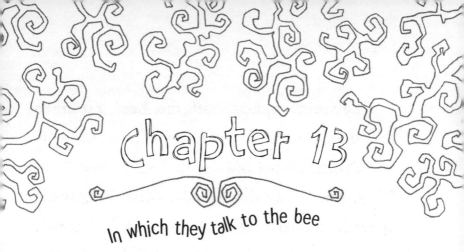

chapter 13

In which they talk to the bee

It was Stewart the Bee. They watched as he made his way across the lawn towards them, swinging a small basket that was full of flowers.

'Hello, Stewart the Bee!' said Ketchup-Face brightly.

Stewart the Bee started in surprise and looked slightly worried. He took a note out of his basket and read it slowly three times. 'Er, yes, that's right, I'm a bee,' he said. 'Hello.'

'Do you know where the other bees are?' Stinkbomb asked him.

'Oh, yes,' said Stewart the Bee. 'I can do that one.' And he began to dance around them, **waggling** his bottom.

'What *are* you doing?' asked King Toothbrush Weasel in astonishment.

'I'm telling you where the other bees are,' said Stewart the Bee happily, **waggling** his bottom and dancing some more.

'No you're not, you silly!' said Ketchup-Face. 'You're just dancing about and **wiggling** your botty!'

Stewart the Bee stopped dancing. 'Yes, but I'm a bee,' he said. Suddenly looking slightly uncertain, he took the note out and checked it again. 'I'm a bee,' he said with more confidence, 'and this is how bees tell other bees where things are. I read it in a book I found in the beehive,' he added proudly.

'There aren't any books in the beehive!' said King Toothbrush Weasel.

'Yes there are,' said Stewart the Bee. 'There's a big bookcase full of them, just next to the throne.'

'But there isn't a throne in the . . . ' King Toothbrush Weasel began; and then he stopped, and looked worried, and said, 'Um, this throne . . . is it trimmed with tinsel?'

'Oh, yes,' said Stewart the Bee.

'And does it have a label on it saying "Throne"?' asked King Toothbrush Weasel.

'Oh, yes,' said Stewart the Bee.

'And is it comfy, in the way that a comfy arm-chair is comfy?' asked King Toothbrush Weasel.

'I expect so,' said Stewart the Bee. 'But I don't know for certain, because Harry the Bee won't let anyone else sit on it.'

'You silly bees!' said King Toothbrush Weasel. 'You've moved into my palace instead of the beehive!'

'Yeah, well,' came a voice from above them; and they turned to see Harry the Bee leaning out of an upstairs window. 'The thing is, the beehive's a bit small, and not very comfy, and we thought it'd be fairer if we swapped.'

'*Swapped?*' said King Toothbrush Weasel indignantly. 'You can't just decide to swap a beehive for my palace! Anyway, palaces are for kings and queens, not bees!'

'Er, well, actually, bees do have queens,' Stink-bomb pointed out.

'Yeah!' said Harry the Bee. 'Bees have queens! Er . . . do they?'

'Yes,' said Stinkbomb. 'Every swarm has a queen bee, and there's a queen bee in every hive. You must have a queen bee, don't you?'

'Er . . . I suppose so,' said Harry the Bee. 'Here! Rolf the Bee!'

'Yes?' said Rolf the Bee, appearing at the window.

'Who's our queen bee, then?'

Rolf the Bee scratched his head. 'Er . . . I suppose that must be you,' he said.

Harry the Bee gave him a hard stare. 'Don't be stupid!' he said. 'I can't be a queen bee. I'm a *boy* bee!'

Rolf the Bee scratched his head again. 'Are you sure?' he asked.

'Of *course* I'm sure!' Harry the Bee said. 'I'm called Harry the Bee, aren't I? And Harry the Bee's a boy bee's name!'

'It might be short for Harriet the Bee,' Rolf the Bee pointed out.

'Fair point,' said Harry the Bee. 'I suppose I'd better check. Um . . . . how *do* you check if you're a boy bee or a girl bee?'

Rolf the Bee whispered something to him.

Harry the Bee's mouth dropped open with shock. 'I'm not looking there!' he said. 'That's rude!!!'

'Well,' said Rolf the Bee slowly, 'if you're not going to check, then you might be a girl bee after all. And if you might be a girl bee, then you might be the queen bee. And if nobody else is the queen bee . . .'

'Then I'd better be the queen bee,' Harry the Bee said quickly, remembering that if he was the queen bee then he got to boss the other bees about and sit on the throne. 'It's all right,' he called down. 'We *do* have a queen bee. I remember now.'

'Even so,' said King Toothbrush Weasel crossly, 'you can't have my palace!' And he strode to the back door, pulled it open, and stepped firmly inside.

Above Stinkbomb and Ketchup-Face, the window closed. A moment later it opened again, and Harry the Bee and Rolf the Bee dangled King Toothbrush Weasel out and dropped him on the rose bed.

'Oof!' said King Toothbrush Weasel.

'Hur hur hur!' said Rolf the Bee.

Stinkbomb looked sharply up at him. 'That was an **evil** and **wicked** laugh, wasn't it?'

'Er . . . no,' said Rolf the Bee. 'I just . . . er . . . I just got a bit of pollen stuck in my throat, that's all.'

'Oh,' said Stinkbomb, in a not-at-all-convinced sort of voice. 'OK.' And they all went round to the front of the palace again, except for Stewart the Bee, who slipped in through the back door and locked it behind him.

At the front of the palace, they found the little shopping trolley waiting patiently. They found Malcolm the Cat asleep on top of his furry bearskin guardsman's hat in his sentry box. They found Ziggy and Wiggo yelping `Badger!` and pulling the furry bearskin guardsman's hat out from underneath Malcolm the Cat.

They did not find Miss Butterworth, because she had mysteriously disappeared as quickly as she had mysteriously appeared, saying something about her lunch hour being over and needing to get back to the library.

King Toothbrush Weasel explained to the others about the bees having moved into the Royal Palace.

'And do you know what,' said Stinkbomb; 'I think those bees might be **evil** and **wicked** bees. I'm sure Rolf the Bee keeps laughing an **evil** and **wicked** laugh.'

Everybody thought about this; and then Ketchup-Face suddenly burst out, 'Wait a minute! If the bees are **evil** and **wicked** bees—maybe it's the bees who have stolen the badgers!'

'Yes,' said Stinkbomb. 'And maybe they've stolen the stripy rugby shirts and fairy wings as well.'

Everybody thought about this, too; and then the little shopping trolley said hesitantly, 'Um

'. . . excuse me . . . but . . . well, how do you know they're bees?'

'Because they're stripy, of course,' said Ketch-up-Face. 'And they've got wings.'

'But if they're already stripy and have got wings,' the little shopping trolley went on, 'why would they want to steal stripy tops and wings?'

'Oh, yeah,' said Stinkbomb. 'Fair point. The bees can't be the criminals after all.'

'Er, that's not what I meant,' said the little shopping trolley. 'I mean . . . maybe they stole the stripy rugby tops and wings to make them look like bees?'

'What,' said Stinkbomb, 'you mean they're not bees at all?'

'Maybe not,' suggested the little shopping trolley shyly.

'But if they're not bees,' said King Toothbrush Weasel, 'who *are* they?'

'Well,' said the little shopping trolley, 'who do we know who are **evil** and **wicked** enough to disguise themselves as bees and take over the palace?'

Everybody scratched their heads and thought for a bit, and then Stinkbomb said, 'Well . . . of course, there's the badgers. But . . . '

'But they can't be the badgers,' Ketchup-Face pointed out, 'because somebody's stolen them.'

'But . . . Well, but what if they *are* the badgers?' the little shopping trolley asked with unaccustomed boldness.

'Hmmm,' said King Toothbrush Weasel. 'What do our experts think?'

'Definitely not badgers,' said Ziggy.

'Nope!' agreed Wiggo

'How do you know?' asked the little shopping trolley.

'Well,' said Ziggy, as if explaining to an idiot, 'they said so.'

'But what if they're lying?' the little shopping trolley asked.

'Ooh,' said Ketchup-Face, rubbing her chin, 'This is all very confusing.'

Ziggy sat down and scratched his head just behind his ear, very quickly. 'Um . . . well, Rolf the Bee has a big badge that says (Big Bee),' he said. 'So he must be a bee.'

'And Harry the Bee has a mug that says World's Best Bee,' Wiggo added. 'So *he* must be a bee.'

'But what if . . . ' Stinkbomb said slowly. 'What if that's just part of the disguise?'

'You mean,' said Ketchup-Face, who had been listening very carefully, 'maybe it was the badgers who stole all the stripy rugby shirts?'

'Could be,' said Stinkbomb.

'And maybe it was the badgers who stole all the dressing-up fairy wings?' said Ketchup-Face.

'Could be,' said Stinkbomb.

'And maybe,' Ketchup-Face went on, following her line of reasoning through to the very end, 'maybe it was the badgers who stole themselves?'

'Er . . . yes,' said Stinkbomb. 'I suppose so.'

Ziggy and Wiggo looked at each other. Then, with a furious yelping of

Badger! Badger! Badger!'

they hurled themselves at the front door of
the palace.

'You can't get in that way,' said King Toothbrush Weasel. 'Why not use the army-flap?'

Ziggy and Wiggo used the army-flap, which
was a little door cut into the bigger door. Immediately, there was the sound of much barking and
scurrying, and then the upstairs window opened

and some bees dropped Ziggy and Wiggo out on top of King Toothbrush Weasel.

'Oof!' said King Toothbrush Weasel.

'Hur hur hur,' laughed Rolf the Bee.

'That does it,' said Stinkbomb. 'That was *definitely* an **evil** and **wicked** laugh. Either you're badgers, or you're **evil** and **wicked** bees.'

'Well, in that case, we're **evil** and **wicked** bees,' said Rolf the Bee. 'Isn't that right, Queen Harry the Bee?'

'Nope,' said Queen Harry the Bee. 'We're badgers.'

'Are we?' said Stewart the Badger, checking his note again.

'Yep,' said Harry the Badger. 'And look what I've found.' He held up a big book called 𝕿𝖍𝖊 𝕲𝖗𝖊𝖆𝖙 𝕶𝖊𝖗𝖋𝖚𝖋𝖋𝖑𝖊 𝕭𝖎𝖌 𝕭𝖔𝖔𝖐 𝖔𝖋 𝕷𝖆𝖜𝖘. 'This,' he went on, 'is where all the laws of Great Kerfuffle are written down. Now we can write our own!'

'You fiends!' cried King Toothbrush Weasel.

'I bet that was your **evil** and **wicked** plan all along, you naughties!' added Ketchup-Face.

'Er . . . no,' said Harry the Badger. 'Our **evil** and **wicked** plan all along was to steal the rugby shirts and fairy wings and pretend to be bees.'

'Yeah!' agreed Rolf the Badger. 'It was a really, really **evil** and **wicked** plan, wasn't it?'

'Not really,' said Stinkbomb. 'As far as **evil** and **wicked** plans go, it was a bit rubbish.'

'Oh,' said Harry the Badger. 'Oh, well. We've got a better **evil** and **wicked** plan now, anyway. We're going to rule the island! Hur hur . . . No, wait, that's Rolf the Badger's **evil** and **wicked** laugh. Which one did I pick?'

'Um . . . I think it was

"Har har har",

said Stewart the Badger helpfully.

'Oh, yeah,' said Harry the Badger.

'Har har har.'

And with that, he opened the book and began to write.

chapter 15

As they watched, Harry the Badger got a pencil and began to rewrite all the laws of Great Kerfuffle. He wrote a law saying that everyone had to put out their dustbins every day, and not just on bin collection day. He wrote a law saying that King Toothbrush Weasel wasn't in charge any more and everyone had to do what the badgers said instead. And then he wrote a law saying that Stinkbomb and Ketchup-Face and King Toothbrush Weasel and Malcolm the Cat and the little shopping trolley and Ziggy and Wiggo had to clear off.

So Stinkbomb and Ketchup-Face and King Toothbrush Weasel and Malcolm the Cat and the little shopping trolley and Ziggy and Wiggo cleared off.

'What are we going to do?'

wailed King Toothbrush Weasel, a little further on.

'Well,' said the little shopping trolley nervously, 'we might consider running away. Look!'

They looked—and froze in horror; for on top of a conveniently-placed hill stood a line of fearsome and menacing figures.

'Badger!'

yelped Wiggo.

'No, you silly!' said Ketchup-Face. 'It's those horrid office chairs!'

As indeed it was. 'Aaargh!' cried the leader, and all the other office chairs yelled 'Aaargh!' in agreement, and then they charged. It was a bloodcurdling sight.

'Oh,' said Stinkbomb. 'Maybe it does do that after all.'

'Maybe what does do what?' Ketchup-Face asked.

'Maybe blood does curdle,' Stinkbomb told her. 'It felt like mine just did.'

'I think mine did, too,' said Ketchup-Face.

And then the chairs surrounded them, and the leader leaned in so close they could smell the leather of his seat, and said:

'Hello.'

'Er . . . hello,' said Stinkbomb nervously.

'We got out of the big hole,' the leader said.

'Er . . . yes, I can see that,' said Stinkbomb.

'And now we're going to take our revenge.'

'How are you going to do that, you naughties?' asked Ketchup-Face defiantly.

'Well,' the leader said turning to King Tooth-brush Weasel, 'we're going to take the kingdom away from you.'

143

'Too late,' said King Toothbrush Weasel sadly. 'The badgers already did that.'

At this, the office chairs roared with frustration. 'Aaaargh!' yelled the leader. 'Thwarted!'

'Oooh,' said Ketchup-Face. 'That's a good word! What does it mean?'

'Well,' said Stinkbomb knowledgeably, 'if you thwart somebody, you stop them from doing something they wanted to do, like taking revenge.'

'Gosh,' said Ketchup-Face. 'So have we thwarted the badgers?'

'Three times now,' said Stinkbomb proudly. 'We haven't thwarted them in this story yet, though.'

'Haven't we?' said Ketchup-Face. 'I think we ought to.'

'Yes,' agreed Stinkbomb, 'but of course the problem is . . . '

'Oi!' said the bandit leader crossly. '*Must* you have these long conversations just when we're being menacing?'

'Oh, sorry,' said Stinkbomb. 'Where were we?'

'The naughty bandits had just been thwarted,' said Ketchup-Face, a little smugly.

'Yes!' agreed the bandit leader crossly; and all the other office chairs went, 'Grrr!' and rattled their little wheels. 'So,' the bandit leader went on, 'what you're saying is: if we want to take the kingdom away from you, we have to take it away from the badgers first, and then give it to you, and then take it away from you again?'

'Um . . . Yes, I suppose so,' agreed King Tooth-brush Weasel uncertainly.

'Honestly,' said the bandit leader. 'These things are never simple, are they? Now we have to find out where the badgers are.'

'And where would that be?' asked King Toothbrush Weasel politely.

'Right here!' said Harry the Badger, who was indeed right there. 'We thought we'd come after Stinkbomb and Ketchup-Face and King Toothbrush Weasel and Malcolm the Cat and the little shopping trolley and Ziggy and Wiggo and make them clear off again, 'cos it was so funny the first time.'

'Yeah,' agreed the other badgers.

The bandit leader rolled menacingly towards Harry the Badger. 'Well, that's lucky,' it said. 'It means we don't have to come and find you.'

'Oh, yeah?' said Harry the Badger. 'And what would you want to come and find us for?'

'So we can take the kingdom off you, of course,' said the bandit leader.

'And what if we don't let you take the kingdom off us?' said Harry the Badger in his best tough-guy voice; and the other badgers laughed their **evil** and **wicked** laughs from *The Big Book of Evil and Wicked Laughs.*

'Then,' said the bandit leader in an even tougher tough-guy voice, 'we're going to subject you to the most fearsome punishment known to furniturekind!' And the other office chairs laughed some **evil** and **wicked** laughs that sounded even more **evil** and **wicked** than the **evil** and **wicked** laughs in *The Big Book of Evil and Wicked Laughs,* because they came from a book called *The Big Book of Evil and Wicked Laughs—New Improved Edition, Now With Even Eviller and Wickeder Evil And Wicked Laughs.*

'Awww,' said all the badgers, feeling rather outdone.

'Well, anyway,' said Harry the Badger, scribbling furiously in **The Great Kerfuffle Big Book of Laws**. 'You can't subject us to the most fearsome punishment known to furniturekind. There's a law against it. So there.'

'Ah,' said the bandit leader. 'But the thing is—we're bandits. We don't care about the law. So there, twice as much as you can ever say and no returns.' And turning to the other bandits, he yelled,

'Get them!'

Harry the Badger turned to the other badgers to say, 'Run!', but the other badgers were already running. So Harry the Badger ran too. And with a dreadful

'Aaargh!!!'

the office chairs gave chase.

'Well,' said King Toothbrush Weasel. 'I'm really not sure what to do now.'

'I think,' said Stinkbomb uncertainly, 'that we ought to go after them and see what happens.'

And they all scrambled into the little shopping trolley, and the little shopping trolley, too, gave chase.

chapter 16

In which there is a terrible battle

'**Wheee!**' shouted Ketchup-Face happily. 'Giddy-up, Starlight!'

The little shopping trolley made no reply, but sped onward in a frantic chase that took them three times round the island and into the little village of Loose Chippings in less than a single sentence.

'Not *again!*' grumped Ketchup-Face.

'It's not over yet!' Stinkbomb pointed out.

'Look!'

Just ahead of them the office chairs, shrieking their bloodcurdling war-cries, were chasing the badgers through the village.

'Quick!' yelled Rolf the Badger. 'In here!'

And the badgers hurled themselves through a heavy iron door and slammed it behind them.

'Oh, good!' said Stinkbomb. 'They've locked themselves in jail again!'

But there was no time for celebration, for at this point the office chairs turned and surrounded them.

'Well,' said the bandit leader, 'with the badgers in prison, all we have to do now is get rid of you lot, and Great Kerfuffle will be ours!

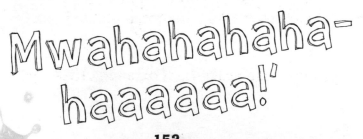

Mwahahahaha-haaaaaa!'

'Gosh,' said Stinkbomb. 'That *is* an impressive **evil** and **wicked** laugh.'

'Do you really think so?' said the bandit leader. 'Thanks!'

'*I* can do an **evil** and **wicked** laugh,' said Ketchup-Face. 'Would you like to hear it?'

'Er, no,' said the bandit leader. 'Because now we're going to get rid of you. Get them!'

And instantly all was chaos as the battle began. There was shouting, and the rattling of tiny wheels, and more shouting.

With a cry of

'Badger!'

Ziggy and Wiggo each leapt on a red office chair.

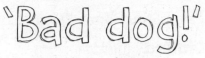

'Bad dog!'

cried the chairs.

'Down! You're not allowed on the furniture!'

Malcolm the Cat jumped onto the badly-cushioned grey chair with the ink-stained seat and began to sharpen his claws on it. 'Ow!' yelped the chair.

The bandit leader scooped up Ketchup-Face. 'Aha!' it cried. 'Got you! Now to subject you to the most fearsome punishment known to furniturekind!'

And it began to spin, faster and faster.

'Wheee!'

Ketchup-Face yelled.

'You're not supposed to go

"Wheee!"'

shouted the bandit leader crossly, spinning
faster still.

'It's a
punishment!!!'

Stinkbomb found himself surrounded by five of
the enemy. As they closed in upon him, he felt fran-
tically in his pockets and pulled out several cans of
air-freshener. Discarding the ones marked 'Mountain Pine', 'Summer Rose', and 'Lemon Burst', he

raised the one labelled 'Accountant's Bottom' and fired.

'Eeeeeugh!' choked the office chairs, backing away.

shouted Ketchup-Face again.

'Faster! Faster!'

Then, as if by magic, Miss Butterworth was there, her big sword drawn and ready. Instantly, she was surrounded by a group of ten green leather-look office chairs, which snarled viciously at her, edging closer.

'*Make your choice!*' commanded Miss Butterworth. '*You can face the fury of my big sword . . . !*'

'Or?' sneered one of the green leather-look office chairs.

'*Or,*' said Miss Butterworth, '*you can have a nice story with Miss Tibbles, who runs Bouncy Sing and Clap Story Time for Toddlers at the library.*'

'I've got a lovely picture book just here,' said Miss Tibbles, popping up next to her. 'It's called *Billy Bunny's Ballet*. Would you like to hear it?'

'Oooh, yes please!' said the green leather-look office chairs, gathering around Miss Tibbles excitedly.

'*Bad dog!!!*' yelled the red office chairs. '*Get off!*'

'Grrr!' replied Ziggy and Wiggo happily, worrying away at the armrests.

Malcolm the Cat, who had curled up on the ink-stained seat of the badly-cushioned grey chair and gone to sleep, snored loudly.

shouted Ketchup-Face.

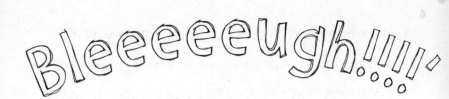

And with that, she was sick all over the bandit leader.

'Oh, *yuk!*' said the bandit leader, stopping suddenly, so that Ketchup-Face was thrown off and landed in the little shopping trolley on top of King Toothbrush Weasel. 'Eeeugh! I'm covered in sick!'

'Eeeeew,' said all the other office chairs, backing away.

'I'll have to go home and have a bath now!' the bandit leader complained.

'Yeah,' agreed another of the outlaws. 'Me too. I smell of dog.'

'And *I* smell like an accountant's bottom,' grumbled a third. 'Again.'

'But what about the battle?' said Harry the Badger, from the safety of the jail. 'We were enjoying that!'

'Yeah,' agreed the other badgers, who had all been pressed against the barred windows, watching. 'It was fun!'

'And what about *Billy Bunny's Ballet?*' asked the green leather-look office chairs.

'Yes,' said Miss Tibbles. 'We were just getting to the best bit.'

'We can't go battling when we smell of sick and dogs and accountants' bottoms,' said the bandit chief. 'We'll go and wash, and then we'll come back and finish the battle, OK?'

And the office chairs turned and rattled off into the coming evening. The badly-cushioned grey chair with the ink-stained seat paused to tip the sleeping Malcolm the Cat into the little shopping trolley's basket.

'Right,' said Harry the Badger. 'You can let us out now.'

'No, you naughty badgers!' Ketchup-Face said. 'You're in jail right where you belong! We're *not* letting you out.'

'Aha!' said Harry the Badger, scribbling furiously in 𝕿𝖍𝖊 𝕲𝖗𝖊𝖆𝖙 𝕶𝖊𝖗𝖋𝖚𝖋𝖋𝖑𝖊 𝕭𝖎𝖌 𝕭𝖔𝖔𝖐 𝖔𝖋 𝕷𝖆𝖜𝖘. 'But you have to! It's the law!'

And he held up 𝕿𝖍𝖊 𝕲𝖗𝖊𝖆𝖙 𝕶𝖊𝖗𝖋𝖚𝖋𝖋𝖑𝖊 𝕭𝖎𝖌 𝕭𝖔𝖔𝖐 𝖔𝖋 𝕷𝖆𝖜𝖘 and showed them where it said:

ALL BADGERS HAVE TO BE LET OUT OF JAIL WHENNEVER THEY ASK, SO THEIR.

'See?' he added.

King Toothbrush Weasel sighed. 'He's right,' he said. 'It's the law!'

'Hang on,' said Stinkbomb. 'It doesn't count if it's spelt wrong.'

'Doesn't it?' said King Toothbrush Weasel and Harry the Badger together.

'No, it doesn't!' Stinkbomb assured them. 'There's a law about it in the book!'

'Is there?' said Harry the Badger, leafing through 𝕮𝖍𝖊 𝕲𝖗𝖊𝖆𝖙 𝕶𝖊𝖗𝖋𝖚𝖋𝖋𝖑𝖊 𝕭𝖎𝖌 𝕭𝖔𝖔𝖐 𝖔𝖋 𝕷𝖆𝖜𝖘. 'I can't find that one!'

'I'll find it for you, if you like!' Stinkbomb offered.

'Oh,' said Harry the Badger. 'OK, thanks!' And he passed 𝕮𝖍𝖊 𝕲𝖗𝖊𝖆𝖙 𝕶𝖊𝖗𝖋𝖚𝖋𝖋𝖑𝖊 𝕭𝖎𝖌 𝕭𝖔𝖔𝖐 𝖔𝖋 𝕷𝖆𝖜𝖘 out through the bars.

Stinkbomb took the book. Then taking a rubber out of his pocket, he rubbed out all the laws the badgers had written, and, taking a pen,

did a bit of writing of his own. Then he showed the
badgers what it said:

Only correctly-spelt laws count.

'Awww!' said all the badgers.

'So you have to stay in there, you naughties!'
said Ketchup-Face cheerfully. 'And give back all
the stripy rugby tops and fairy wings!'

'Awww!' said the badgers again, tak-
ing off the stripy rugby tops and fairy wings and
passing them out through the bars as well.

'And since the army is still asleep at his post,'
said King Toothbrush Weasel, 'I think we ought to
ask Ziggy and Wiggo to guard the jail.'

'Us?' asked Ziggy. 'Why us?'

'Well,' explained the king, 'because it's full of badgers.'

Ziggy's and Wiggo's eyes opened wide. '*Is* it?' they asked, and they looked suspiciously at the badgers. 'They don't *look* like badgers!'

'Well,' said Ketchup-Face happily, 'they are. So there.'

Ziggy's and Wiggo's eyes opened even wider. They stared at the contents of the jail for a moment. And then Wiggo yelped, 'Badger!' and an instant later both dogs were yelping

'Badger! Badger!

Badger!'

and doing excited little jumps at the door.

'Gaaaah!' said Harry the Badger crossly. 'We'll get out again. And just watch out when we do, that's all!'

'Come on, everyone,' said King Toothbrush Weasel. 'For some reason, I really fancy a honey sandwich—and I know just the place to get one.'

'And where would that be?' asked Stinkbomb and Ketchup-Face politely.

@ @ @

And so, minutes later, they were all gathered round a table in the Loose Chippings Cafe, enjoying some delicious honey sandwiches. It felt warm and cosy, just the way the end of an adventure should feel. Only one more thing, Stinkbomb and Ketchup-Face thought, was needed to make the scene completely perfect.

And then, to their delight, they saw two famil-
iar shapes silhouetted once more on the frosted
glass of the cafe door, and the door began to open.

'Mum! Dad!' cried Stinkbomb.

'HELLO, MY DARLINGS!'

came their mother's voice from outside.

'CAN WE COME IN? HAS THE STORY FINISHED YET?'

'Yes,' said Ketchup-Face happily.

'Aaaargh!' roared the bandit leader, appearing suddenly, with his fearsome gang of office chairs behind him and roaring

'Aaaaargh!'

as well.

Then they stopped, and looked around. 'Er, where is everybody?' the bandit leader asked. 'We're supposed to be finishing a terrible battle.'

'You're too late,' said the caretaker. 'The story's over, and everyone's gone home. I'm just about to lock up.'

'But what about the terrible battle?' the bandit leader said indignantly.

'You'll have to finish it another time,' said the caretaker. 'And by the way, it was a terrible battle. It was absolutely rubbish. I've read *lots* of books with battles in, and that was definitely the worst battle I've ever read.'

'Hmmmph,' hmmphed the bandit leader. Then it looked more closely at the caretaker. 'Wait a minute,' it said. 'You're a rat, aren't you?'

'Well, yeah,' admitted the rat. 'The real caretaker's at an after-school club.'

And then the office chairs went home, and the rat locked up the story.

How to Dance Like a Bee!

with Ketchup-Face

Hello! ...

I like bees. They're all little and furry and buzzy, a bit like tiny electric kittens. And they get nectar and pollen from flowers. Which I think is probably like chocolate for bees. Or maybe ketchup.

The bee gets the nectar and pollen by climbing into the flowers. Then it goes home with nectar and pollen all over its face, and does a funny wiggly dance. The dance tells the other bees where the flowers are, so they can all go and get some nectar and pollen all over their faces, too.

This means that bee parties are a bit rubbish, because almost as soon as one bee starts dancing all the other bees fly away. Then they come back and shout things like 'THERE WEREN'T ANY FLOWERS WHERE YOU SAID, YOU STUPID BEE!'.

I'm going to teach you to dance like a bee now. And then you can do a bee dance for all the other bees and it'll be brilliant.

1. If you're going to dance like a bee it's a good idea to look like a bee. So first you need to put on something stripy, like a stripy rugby top or a stripy dress or a stripy policeman's uniform. If you can find a pair of trousers with a spike sticking out of the bottom, that'd be good too. And some wings. And if you can, make yourself really, really small and learn to fly.

2. Then you need to find some flowers. If you did manage to make yourself really, really small you have to climb inside the flowers. Otherwise you can just stick your nose in them.

3. Then you need some other bees to do your dance to. You could ask your mum and dad. They'll probably be bees for a minute, if they're not in the middle of doing emails or cooking the dinner or any of the other boring things that parents love doing all the time. I bet they won't put on stripy tops and wings and spiky trousers, though. Parents are like that.

4. Then you can do your dance. It's great fun. All you do is dance round in a sort of figure-of-eight, wiggling your bottom all over the place and shouting, 'Botty! Botty! Botty!!!!!'

(Stinkbomb doesn't think that bees shout 'Botty! Botty! Botty!!!!!' but I bet they do. I bet that buzzing noise they make is just their way of shouting 'Botty! Botty! Botty!!!!!' I mean, what's the point in wiggling your botty about if you can't shout 'Botty! Botty! Botty!!!!!')

Botty! Botty! Botty!!!!!

5. Anyway, keep doing that until the other bees go and find the flowers. And if they can't find the flowers then say, 'WHAT SORT OF STUPID BEES ARE YOU IF YOU CAN'T EVEN FIND THE FLOWERS AFTER I'VE DONE MY AMAZING DANCE TO TELL YOU WHERE THEY ARE? NOW YOU HAVE TO GIVE ME A HONEY SANDWICH!' And then take them to the flowers and say, 'LOOK! SEE? THEY'RE RIGHT WHERE MY DANCE SAID THEY'D BE!

NOW WHERE'S MY HONEY SANDWICH????'

6. When the other bees have given you the honey sandwich, make sure you dance around while you eat it, wiggling your bottom and shouting, 'Botty! Botty! Botty!!!!!'

Acknowledgements

Thanks to the very lovely Jo Cotterill,
for being my friend when I needed it most.

Thanks too to all my friends from Original Sing
(www.originalsing.co.uk)
— Dave, David, Fi, Gill, Hilary, Kerry, Lisa,
Mel, Peter, Sue & Rob.

Special thanks to Jo McAndrews
for getting the badgers out of jail.

And as always, with grateful thanks to all
the children who have inspired various bits of
silliness in the story, particularly Noah & Cara.
It's all your fault, really.

Photo © Michael Dannenberg

John Dougherty
(Author)

I can write about Stinkbomb and Ketchup-face with one hand tied behind my back!

Illustration by Stanley Tazzyman

David Tazzyman
(Illustrator)

I can draw badgers with my eyes closed!